PATRICIA LEE GAUCH

Tanya and Emily
in a Dance for Two

ILLUSTRATED BY SATOMI ICHIKAWA

PHILOMEL BOOKS • NEW YORK

Text copyright © 1994 by Patricia Lee Gauch. Illustrations copyright © 1994 by Satomi Ichikawa.
Published by Philomel Books, a division of The Putnam & Grosset Group, 200 Madison Avenue, New York, NY 10016.
All rights reserved. This book, or parts thereof, may not be reproduced in any form without permission in writing from
the publisher. Philomel Books, Reg. U.S. Tm. & Pat. Off. Printed in Hong Kong by South China Printing Co. (1988), Ltd.
Book design by Gunta Alexander. The text is set in Horley Old Style.
Library of Congress Cataloging-in-Publication Data
Gauch, Patricia Lee. Tanya and Emily in a dance for two / Patricia Lee Gauch; [illustrated by] Satomi Ichikawa.
p. cm. Summary: When Tanya, the smallest and wiggliest girl in her ballet class, makes friends
with a talented newcomer, they both learn something. [1. Ballet dancing—Fiction. 2. Friendship—Fiction.]
I. Ichikawa, Satomi, ill. II. Title. PZ7.G2315Tan 1994 [E]—dc20 93-5354 CIP AC
ISBN 0-399-22688-5
1 3 5 7 9 10 8 6 4 2
First Impression

For Claudine Allegra—S.I.
and Muriel—P.L.G.

Tanya was a dancer all the time. She danced to the table for supper and under the covers at night. She danced down the sidewalk to class and right through the park.

Since she was the smallest and wiggliest, she was always at the end of the line in class. That was just fine with Tanya. The positions hummed in her head: first position, second position, *saut de chat*, saut de chat, saut de chat.

Then Emily joined the class. Emily was a ballerina in every way.

She stood straight and tall like a ballerina, limbered up like a ballerina. She even walked to the barre like a ballerina.

And, oh, how she could dance. *Arabesque,
jeté, pirouette.* She could even do a *cabriole.*
Never had Tanya done a cabriole.

"A prima ballerina!" Tanya's ballerina bear, Barbara, whispered. Tanya knew she was right. Emily was wonderful.

But Emily was always alone and Tanya was always going her own way, until one day after class when Tanya took the path through the park.

"What are you doing?" Emily asked. "A jeté?"

"No," said Tanya, "an ostrich." And Tanya danced an ostrich.

Tanya ran to the next fence. "An *equilibre*?" said Emily.
"A flamingo!" called Tanya and she was a flamingo.

Now Emily ran ahead. "A penguin!" she said and she danced a penguin.

Tanya danced a leopard.

And Emily danced an antelope.

Emily particularly liked the antelope.

Then they ran to the other end of the park, laughing,
where they danced the giraffe together.

When they stopped to catch their breath,
Emily said, "And now for a cabriole!"
"Show me," Tanya said.

"A wild goat, Tanya. A leaping, wild goat!" Emily said.
And she danced a cabriole right across a hill.

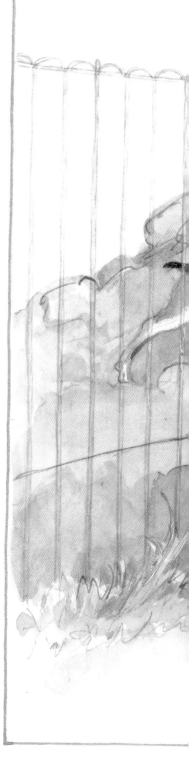

And Tanya did, too.
"Bravo," said Barbara.

After that Emily was not always alone, and Tanya was not always going her own way. Sometimes Emily and Tanya danced to class together. Sometimes they danced home together.

And sometimes they practiced together, laughing together, too.
And their teacher Miss Bessinger noticed.

In the winter recital, at the end when nearly all the dances were over, Miss Bessinger announced, "And now for a *pas de deux*!" And two dancers danced right out of the line.

They danced arabesques and saut de chats, jetés and
one cabriole.

And together they were wonderful.